It was hot and still. Far off, a dust devil danced among the Galleta grass and the creosote brush, but I saw no dust of human make. It could be I'd shaken them. Maybe we would have no trouble after all.

What made me turn my head I'll never know, but glancing over my left shoulder I caught just a glimpse of a rifle muzzle as somebody drew sight on me.

Mister, I left off of that rock like I was taking a free dive into a swimmin' hole, and I hit that heaped-up sand on my shoulder and rolled over. When I came up it was on one knee, the other leg stretched out ahead of me, and my Winchester coming up to firing position . . .

Bantam Books by Louis L'Amour
Ask your bookseller for the books you have missed

Louis L'Amour
Mojave Crossing

BANTAM BOOKS
TORONTO · NEW YORK · LONDON · SYDNEY

MOJAVE CROSSING

A Bantam Book | January 1964

2nd printing .... August 1968	*4th printing .... June 1970*
3rd printing .... August 1968	*5th printing .. September 1970*

New Bantam edition | April 1971

2nd printing .... June 1971	*11th printing .. February 1977*
3rd printing .... October 1971	*12th printing . September 1977*
4th printing .. February 1972	*13th printing .... April 1978*
5th printing .... July 1972	*14th printing . December 1978*
6th printing .... January 1973	*15th printing .... January 1979*
7th printing ...... August 1973	*16th printing .... January 1979*
8th printing .... July 1974	*17th printing .... May 1979*
9th printing . December 1974	*18th printing .... May 1980*
10th printing .. February 1976	*19th printing .... June 1980*

20th printing .... February 1981

Photograph of Louis L'Amour
by John Hamilton—Globe Photos, Inc.

Library of Congress Catalog Card Number: 64-10937

ISBN 0–553–20075–5

Published simultaneously in the United States and Canada

*Bantam Books are published by Bantam Books, Inc. Its trade-
mark, consisting of the words "Bantam Books" and the por-
trayal of a bantam, is Registered in U.S. Patent and Trademark
Office and in other countries. Marca Registrada. Bantam
Books, Inc., 666 Fifth Avenue, New York, New York 10103.*

to Parker

Mojave Crossing

one

When I saw that black-eyed woman a-looking at me I wished I had a Bible.

There I was, a big raw-boned mountain boy, rougher than a cob and standing six feet three inches in my socks, with hands and shoulders fit to wrassle mustang broncs or ornery steers, but no hand with womenfolks.

Nobody ever claimed that I was anything but a homely man, but it was me she was looking at in that special way she had.

Where we Sacketts come from in the high-up mountains of Tennessee, it is a known thing that if you sleep with a Bible under your pillow it will keep you safe from witches. Before they can do aught to harm you they must count every word in the Bible, and they just naturally can't finish that before daybreak, when they lose their power to hurt.

Yet when I taken a second look at that black-eyed, black-haired woman I thought maybe it was me should do the counting. She was medium tall, with a way about her that set a man to thinking thoughts best kept to himself. She had the clearest, creamiest

1

skin you ever did see, and a mouth that fairly prickled the hair on the back of your neck.

Most of my years I'd spent shying around in the mountains or out on the prairie lands, with no chance to deal myself any high cards in society, but believe me, there's more snares in a woman's long lashes than in all the creek bottoms of Tennessee. Every time I taken my eyes from that black-haired witch woman it was in me to look back.

My right boot-toe was nudging the saddlebags at my feet, warning me I'd no call to take up with any woman, for there were thirty pounds of gold in those bags, not all of it mine.

The worst of it was, I figured things were already shaping for trouble. Three days hard-running I'd seen dust hanging over my back trail like maybe there was somebody back there who wanted to keep close to me without actually catching up. And that could only mean that trouble lay ahead.

Now, I'm no man who's a stranger to difficulty. No boy who walked out of Tennessee to fight for the Union was likely to be, to say nothing of all that had happened since. Seemed like trouble dogged my tracks wherever I put a foot down, and here was I, heading into strange country, running into a black-eyed woman.

She sat alone and ate alone, so obviously a lady that nobody made a move to approach her. This was a rough place in rough times, but a body would have thought she was setting up to table in Delmonico's or one of those fancy eastern places, her paying no mind to anything or anybody. Except, occasionally, me.

She wasn't all frills and fuss like a fancy woman, for she was dressed simple, but her clothes were made from rich goods. Everything about her warned me I'd best tuck in my tail and skedaddle out of there whilst I was able, for trouble doesn't abide only with fancy women. Even a good woman, with her ways and notions, can cause a man more trouble than he can shoot his way out of, and I'd an idea this here was no good woman.

Trouble was, there just was no place to run to.

Hardyville was little else but a saloon, a supply store, and a hotel at the crossing of the Colorado. Most of the year it was the head of navigation on the river, but there had been a time or two when steamboats had gone on up to the mines in Eldorado Canyon, or even to Callville.*

Come daybreak, I figured to cross the river on the first ferry and take out for the Bradshaw Road and Los Angeles, near the western ocean. It was talked among the Arizona towns that speculators out there would pay eighteen, maybe twenty dollars an ounce for gold, whilst in the mining camps a body could get but sixteen.

It was in my mind to sell my gold in Los Angeles, buy goods and mules, pack across the Mojave Desert and the Colorado, and sell my goods in the mining towns. With luck I'd show profit on my gold, and on my goods as well.

Nobody ever claimed I was any kind of a businessman, least of all me, but if a body can buy cheap and sell high he just naturally ain't liable to starve. Of course, in all things there was a reason, and in this case it was the difficulty of getting either gold or goods through a country full up with outlaws and Indians. Whilst no businessman, I was pretty fair at getting from here to yonder, so I just bowed my neck and plunged in, figuring wherever a body could go a Smoky Mountain Sackett could go.

Speaking rightly, there were three kinds of Sack-

---

*Now under the waters of Lake Mead.

etts in Tennessee. The Smoky Mountain Sacketts, the Cumberland Gap Sacketts, and the Clinch Mountain Sacketts. These here last ones, they were a mean outfit and we had no truck with them unless at feuding time, when we were always pleased to have them on our side, for they were mean men in any kind of a shindig. But most of the time we held off from those Clinch Mountain boys.

There were some lowland Sacketts, too, living in the Cumberland Valley, but they were rich Sacketts and we paid them no mind. Pa, he always said we shouldn't hold it against them if they had money; chances were they couldn't he'p it, no ways.

All the Sacketts, even those no-account Sacketts from Clinch Mountain, run to boy-children. They had a saying over yonder that if you flung a stone into the brush you'd hit a Sackett boy, and likely, although it wasn't said, a Trelawney girl. I don't know what we Sackett boys would have done without the Trelawney girls.

But the only thing I was thinking of now was getting my old saddlebags across the Mojave and to Los Angeles, selling as well as I could, buying as cheap as possible, and getting back to the mines.

Now, when a beautiful woman or a handsome man receives attention it is taken as a matter of course; but I was a plain man, so when this black-eyed woman started paying me mind, I checked my hole card.

Not that I'd lacked for attention where women were concerned . . . not, at least, after they came to know me. Nor could it be said that I was downright distrustful of folks. There's a-plenty of just people in the world, but the flesh is weak and man is prone to sin . . . especially if a woman is involved.

But I was packing gold, and it came upon me to realize there is something about the presence of gold

4

that is favorable to the breathing of beautiful women. And likely this woman, with her witch-black eyes, could see right through the leather of my saddlebags.

Only I'd been storing up pleasure for myself in thinking of a time when I could set up to table and eat a hot meal I hadn't fixed for myself, and sleep in a bed, if only for the strangeness of it. And if I high-tailed it out of here now I'd miss both.

For the life of me I couldn't imagine what a woman like this was doing in Hardyville. By the looks of her, she had come upriver on a steamboat, for her clothes showed no dust, as they would had she come by stage or wagon.

When the waitress brought my food the black-eyed woman stopped her, and asked, "Isn't it time for the stage for Los Angeles?"

"Have to get them a new stage," I said.

"What do you mean?"

"It ain't a-comin' in."

All of them were looking at me now, so I said, "Seen it back yonder." I was buttering a thick slab of bread. "He who was driving is dead . . . two holes alongside his spine. The stage is laying over in the canyon and the horses gone. Two other dead men . . . passengers."

"Are you sure?" This was Hardy asking.

"The buzzards were."

"You didn't go down to them?"

"Not for more'n a minute or two. No tellin' who was laying up in the rocks with a Winchester."

"Mojaves," somebody said, "or Hualapais."

"They wore moccasins, all right, but they weren't Indians. They were Comanche moccasins, and there's no Comanches out here."

Everybody started talking all to once and I set to eating, glad to be let alone. Anyway, it was likely I'd already talked too much. One of those men who'd done the shooting might be right here in this room, although I'd cast eyes about for moccasins when I first came in, habit-like. Seems to me a man has trouble enough in this world without borrowing more with careless words.

That black-eyed woman was talking to the waitress. "But if that stage has been wrecked, how long will it be before there's another?"

"Ma'am, you'll just have to abide. The next regular stage is Thursday."

This here was Monday, and I could see from that woman's face that she had to be shut of Hardyville long before that. And it wasn't just that this was a jumping-off place—she was scared.

That witch woman's lips turned pale and her black eyes grew large, like she'd seen a ghost. Maybe her own.

She turned sharp around to me and said, "Will you take me to Los Angeles with you?"

And me, like a damned fool, and without thinking, I said, "Yes."

It never does any good for a man to cuss himself, unless maybe it helps to impress on his mind what a fool he's been, but right then and there I did a fair to middling job of cussing myself out for seven kinds of a fool. Here I was, in a running hurry to get to Cailifornia—to Los Angeles, that is—and I'd burdened myself with a woman. And by the look of her she'd need coddling.

Well, I'd been fool enough for one day, and maybe I could get out of this yet. "You'll need horses," I said. "Are you packing much gear?"

"My trunk can come by stage. All I'll need will be the two carpetbags."

"My pack horse can handle them if they aren't heavy," I said, "but you'll need two ridin' horses. This here's a fast trip I'm makin'."

"Thank you," she said. "If you will get them for me, I'll pay you in Los Angeles. All I have"—she smiled beautifully—"is my stage ticket and a bank draft too large to cash here."

"I—" I started to object that I didn't have the money, but those saddlebags were pushing at my toe and I'd a sneaking feeling—with no reason for it that I could make sense out of—that she knew what was in those bags.

"All right," I said, and lost my last chance to back out of it.

No getting around it, I was upset. It was my notion to make a fast trip to Los Angeles, which was my reason for two horses, switching from one to the other. Now I had that woman to care for, and no telling what she was like on a horse.

Taking another fill of coffee from the pot on the table, I happened to look across at the bar. A man standing there was looking my way and listening to two others. There seemed to be something familiar about the biggest of them. He was a man as tall as I was, and some heavier. He was a dark, strong-looking man who wore a gun like a man who could use it. His back was to me, and he had a fine set of shoulders on him . . . he was built like a man who could punch.

That woman hadn't moved, and our tables were only two feet apart. Best thing was to get it settled right off.

"If you ride with me," I said, and I'm afraid my tone was kind of rough, "you will be ready to go, come daybreak . . . and that doesn't mean sun-up. It means the first gray in the sky."

Shoving back my chair, I got up. "Can you use a gun?"

Well, sir, she surprised me. "Yes," she said, "I can handle a rifle." And then she smiled at me, and

7

you've never seen such a smile. "And please do not disturb yourself. I shall be no trouble to you."

Fishing those saddlebags off the floor with my left hand, I stood up, dropping a quarter on the table for my meal. Then I taken up my Winchester with my right hand and walked to the door.

A voice spoke behind me, and I had a feeling the big man had turned to look, and I knew that voice was an invitation to turn around, an invitation to trouble. Stepping outside, I closed the door behind me and stood alone in the soft desert night.

It was very still. The Colorado River rustled by out there in the darkness, and beyond the river loomed the Dead Mountains. Over there a narrow point of Nevada came down to join borders with California.

Uneasily, I looked westward into those miles of desert, and the hunch rode my shoulders that I'd see blood and grief before those miles were behind me. A fool I was to entangle myself with that black-eyed woman.

Of a sudden I realized the thing I'd ought to do was to leave now. True, the ferry was not operating, but swimming the river at this point was no new thing. Beale had done it with his camels, and fine swimmers they proved to be.

There was a light in the window of Hardy's cabin. Crossing to it, I tapped on the door, not too loud.

Being a wise man, he spoke before opening the door, but when I told I wanted to make a dicker on some horses, he opened up, but he held a pistol in his hand, which surprised me none at all.

"Yes," he replied, when I had explained myself. "I've two good horses, but they'll cost you."

He slid his gun into its holster and picked up his coat. He started to put it on, then stopped and looked over at me. "Are you taking that Robiseau woman out of here?"

"I never asked her name, nor she mine. She wishes to go to Los Angeles, and I'm riding that way."

He shrugged into his coat. "You're borrowing trouble. Look, I don't know you. You just drifted in here out of nowhere, but that woman is running from something, and whatever it is or whoever it is will bundle you into her package. I mean, they'll resent interference."

"Whatever it is," I said, "she's a woman alone, and needs help."

He didn't say any more, but led the way to the stable and lighted a lantern. The horses in their stalls rolled their eyes at me. There were only a few stalls, for his own good stock. The mustang stuff was in the corrals out back.

One of the two horses he showed me was a liver-colored stallion with a white nose and three white stockings; a long-barreled animal built for speed and staying power, and one of the finest-looking horses I'd seen, and big for this country. It would weigh a good thousand pounds and maybe a mite over. The other horse was a short-coupled gelding, mouse-colored, with a fine head and powerful hindquarters. It was somewhat smaller than the other, but all horse.

We dickered there by lantern light, but he knew I had to have those horses, and he got his price. Yet high as they came, they were worth every penny of it. He had bought them from an Army officer who was changing station. The horses had been the officer's private mounts, and the smaller one had been broken for a woman to ride.

"You made a good buy," Hardy acknowledged,

"although I got my price. There's no better horses around, unless it's those you've got."

We stood in the stable door, listening to the river. "She came up on the boat," Hardy volunteered, "and just missed the stage to Prescott."

"Prescott?"

"Uh-huh. Then she changed her mind and decided on Los Angeles. Seems to me like she wants the first stage out, no matter where it goes."

He paused and we stood there in silence, with me thinking about that road west, and those men who had been following me.

There'd been a time, back along the trail, when I was not sure . . . maybe they were just traveling the same way . . . but when I left Beale's Springs I headed up to the Coyote Wells and got in there with time to spare. Those riders never showed up, although I'd seen their dust on my trail. That could mean only one thing—they were lying out in the hills, making dry camp, just so's I wouldn't see them.

Short of midnight I had left my fire burning low, saddled up, and taken off across the hills. My trail led west, toward Union Pass; but I got a notion, and after whipsawing back and forth in the trail, I cut off through the brush toward the south. South, then west, and through Secret Pass.

At Secret Spring I made camp and slept until well past daybreak. Then, after saddling up, I had climbed to the top of the cliff and looked off to the east and north. Sure enough, there was dust and movement on my back trail. Through my field glasses—taken off a dead Confederate officer on the battlefield—I could just make out four riders.

They had ridden on by the place where I'd turned off, discovering too late that I'd cut out somewhere. Now they were scouting their back trail to find the turn-off. They were a good ten, twelve miles off and in the bottom of Sacramento Wash.

Descending to my outfit, I had mounted up and followed the Secret Pass trail into Hardyville.

Nobody had ridden in, so they were lying out again, fearful of being seen by me, which might mean that I knew them and they feared recognition.

"Whoever it is," Hardy said now, "who wants that Robiseau woman, he wants her pretty bad, and wants her himself."

There was meaning in the way he said it, and I turned to look at him. "Keep out of it, friend," Hardy went on. "Three of those men in the saloon are watching her for somebody, and they shape up like grief a-plenty for anybody in their way."

"I gave her my word."

"Your funeral."

"Maybe," I said gloomily. "I'm not a trouble-hunting man. Not a one of us Sacketts ever was."

Hardy gave a quick, funny sort of sound. "Did you say *Sackett*? Is your name *Sackett*?"

"Sure . . . do you know the name?"

He turned away from me. "Get out . . . get out while you can."

He started off, walking very fast, but when he had taken but a couple of steps he turned around. "Does she know your name? Have you told her that?"

"No . . . no, I never did, come to think on it."

"Of course not . . . of course." He looked at me, but I could not see the expression in his eyes. There was only light enough to see his face under the brim of his hat. "Take my advice and don't tell her . . . not, at least, until you reach Los Angeles—if you do."

He walked away, leaving me almighty puzzled, but convinced the time to leave was now.

11

two

When I looked into the window of the saloon the men at the bar were still drinking their liquor and talking it up. The black-eyed woman was gone.

The hotel had only four special rooms and I had latched onto one of those. The only other occupied one was the one given to the Robiseau girl, so I slipped in the back door and went to her room and tapped ever so gently.

There was a quick rustle of clothing inside, and something that sounded like a click of a drawed-back gun-hammer, and then her voice, low. "I have a pistol. Go away."

"Ma'am," I whispered right back to her, "you want to go to Los Angeles, you come to this door, an' quick."

She came, easing it open a crack. The pistol looking through the opening was no feisty little-girl pistol. It was a sure enough he-coon of a pistol, a .44 Navy Colt.

"Ma'am, if you want to get to Los Angeles, you get dressed. We're leaving out of here in twenty minutes."

I'll give her this—she didn't say aye, yes, or no, she just lowered that gun muzzle and said, "I'll be ready. At the stable?"

"The ferry," I said, "only we're going to swim it. The ferry stopped crossing at sundown."

I'd never left hold of my gold, nor my rifle, but I stepped across the hall and picked up the rest of my gear, took one longing look at that bed, and then tiptoed down the hall and out to the stable.

When I made my dicker for the horses I'd gotten an old saddle thrown in, and now I saddled up two horses.

We'd be riding those two, and leading two spare saddle horses and my pack horse. By swapping horses, we could make faster time than most anybody coming after us, and I was figuring on that.

But that wasn't the only bee I had in my bonnet. True it was that I'd never ridden those westward trails that lay before us, but I'd listened to a sight of talk about them from those who had, and it came over me that a body might strike off on a new route and make it through, if he was lucky.

That would be something to keep in mind.

She was at the river, carpetbags and all, when I got there with the horses. She had dressed in an all-fired hurry, but she didn't show it. Helping her into the saddle, I got the feel of her arm, and she was all woman, that one. She swung up, hooking one knee around the horn like she was riding a sidesaddle, and we taken off.

The water was dark, and there was more current than a body would expect. Walking our horses into the water, I pointed across. "Make for that peak, and when you get over there, don't call out. If we get separated, just stay put. I'll find you."

Holding my rifle and gunbelt high, I rode on into the water, and she followed.

I felt the stallion's feet go out from under him as he hit deep water.

He was a strong swimmer, and when I glanced back I saw that woman right behind me, her horse swimming strong too. We made it up the bank, and as I turned to glance back I heard a door slam and somebody shouted and swore.

"What the hell?" I said. "They ain't found out a-ready?"

She pulled up beside me. "Maybe the ferryman told them," she said.

"*Ferryman?* How would he know?"

She turned and looked at me like I was a fool. "Why, I asked him to take us across. He refused."

Me, I'd never hit a woman, but I wanted to right then. I wanted to hit her the worst way. Instead, I just turned my horse and started off into the Dead Mountains, mad enough to tackle a grizzly with my bare hands.

"Ma'am," I said roughly, "you played hell. The reason we started now was to get some distance between us before daylight. Now you've tipped them off and they will be comin' right behind us."

"But they couldn't!" she protested. "He's not—I mean, why would anybody want to catch us?"

"You know that better than me, but even Hardy knew some of those men back at the saloon were there to watch you. He told me so."

She shut up then, having nothing more to say and no chance to say it, for I led off, walking that stallion fast. Having the fresh horse was going to spell my two horses, and they could use the rest.

The trail lay white under the hoofs of the horses; the desert night was still. That liver-colored stallion went out of there like he had a fire under his tail, and I'll hand it to that black-eyed girl. No matter how she had to sit her saddle, she stayed with me.

15

No telling what those men wanted with her, but in these times there were white men with bloodier hands than any Indian, and I was asking for no trouble I could avoid with honor. Just short of daylight I drew up and we swapped saddles to fresh horses, but it was an hour later before I made my move.

The Dead Mountains lay behind us and I turned up a dry wash. If my memory was working along the lines of what I'd been told, this was Piute Wash and it ran due north for quite a spell, then a dim trail would cut over toward Piute Spring.

There was no time for talk, and I had no mind for it, wanting only to put distance between myself and those men back there. They might run us down, or they might wait until the steamboat came in with whoever was on it.

At Piute Spring, on the eastern foot of the range, we pulled up long enough to water the horses and drink a mite ourselves. The valley ahead of us was mostly flat-seeming land covered with Joshua trees. We went out of the shadow of the Piute Range and into the Joshuas, and at first they were scattered, then they thickened up. Once into the Joshuas, we slowed down to raise as little dust as possible.

There were thousands of those trees there in the valley, and they offered a might of cover. From a height, somebody might have picked us out, but nobody on our own level was likely to, so we pushed on, holding parallel to the old Government Road from Fort Mojave.

The sun had gone before we sighted the draw I was looking for and, riding up a hundred yards, came to Rock Spring. There was little water, which suited me, for when we left I didn't mean for there to be any.

The Robiseau woman looked pale and drawn when

I reached up to take her by the waist to swing her down. Tired as she was, she wasn't ready to haul down her flag. As her feet touched the ground she let her hands rest on my forearms and said, "You're very strong."

"I'd better be."

She gave me an odd look, but I turned away and began gathering sticks for a fire. The spot was sheltered, and there was time for coffee and a quick meal.

This was something I'd done so often that it was no trick at all, and by the time I'd stripped the saddles the water was boiling and the food about ready.

"You haven't told me your name."

"Folks call me Tell."

"Only that?"

"It's enough."

"I am Dorinda Robiseau."

It sounded like a made-up name, but I'd known folks with real names that sounded made up. "Pleased to meet you."

"You haven't asked me why I couldn't wait for the stage."

"Your business."

She acted like she wanted to explain, but I had no plan to get more involved than I was. I'd been fool enough to take her along, but the sooner I got shut of her the better.

Sitting under the stars, we ate a quick meal, then finished the coffee I'd made. "There's something about a campfire . . ." she said. "I like to look into the coals."

"Take your last look," I said. "I'm putting it out." When I'd kicked sand over the coals I added, "Fool thing, looking into a fire. When you look away you're blind . . . and men have been killed thataway."

17

I saddled up and loaded our packs. She looked like she couldn't believe what I was doing, but I said, "If you're coming with me, get up in the saddle."

"You're going on? *Tonight?*"

"You want your friends to catch us? You can bet if I knew where this spring was, they'll know. In the desert a man's travelin' is pretty well cut and dried by where he can find water."

Whoever those men were, they must be wanting her pretty bad to follow us as they were. Of course, there was a chance they were following *me*. They might be the same outfit that had trailed me to Hardyville. There'd been a bunch of renegades drifting through the country raiding ranches or mine prospects for supplies. Somebody said they were a Frisco outfit that had come down through Nevada.

As for this Robiseau girl, she might be somebody's wife, or she might have been involved in some shady doings out California way. Anyway, they needed her bad enough to chase her.

Meanwhile, I'd been doing some pondering of the situation, and there was nothing about it to make a man content. According to what I'd been told when preparing to start westward, it was twenty miles to the next water at Marl Spring, almost due west of where we were now. Most of that twenty miles lay out on bare desert, and if we started from here now we could make it by daylight—if we didn't stray from the trail.

If we strayed . . . Well, there were bones a-plenty out there on the desert to answer that question. Moreover, I had me a tired woman, in no shape for such a ride.

In those days every saloon was a clearing house for information. Sitting around in a saloon or standing at a bar, loafing in a cow camp or riding the trail, men just naturally talked about places they'd been. It was likely to be all a body would ever get to know about trails or towns until he traveled them, so men listened and remembered.

Nobody reckoned in miles. Not often, at least. Distance was reckoned in time, and a place was a day's ride, or two days' ride, or whatever.

And many a cowhand who had never left Texas could describe in detail the looks of Hickok, Earp, Tilghman, Masterson, or Mathers. If a body wasn't able to recognize the town marshal, he'd best not try to cut any fancy didoes in western towns.

So I knew a good bit about the Mojave, although I'd not crossed it before. I knew what landmarks to look for, and the trouble to expect. Only nobody had told me I'd be crossing the wide sand with a fine-dressed woman behind me.

Well, it was twenty miles to water if I held to the trail, but there was water south along the Providence Mountains, and if we could locate one of those springs we could hole up for the night, then work our way south. We'd be taking big risks, venturing off into the desert thataway, but there was a good chance we'd leave all pursuit behind.

And so it was that when we left out of Rock Spring, we headed south.

The night, as desert nights are inclined to be, was cool . . . almost cold. There were many stars, and around us lifted the jagged shoulders of black, somber-looking mountains. We went at an easy pace, the ground being rough and the country unfamiliar, and we had to pick our way. So it was over an hour of riding before we covered the six miles to Black Canyon.

There was a spring in the canyon, but we took no time to look for it, pushing on toward the south.

Getting through the canyon, which was close to impassable, was a struggle. By daylight it might have been no trouble, but at night it used up time, and by the time we covered the four additional miles to Granite Well, we were tuckered.

We made dry camp a short way from the well, bedding down on a patch of drift sand among the rocks. Rolling out my bed, I pointed at it. "You roll up there. I'll sleep on the sand."

"I've no right to take your bed."

"Don't argue," I said shortly. "I can't have you falling out of the saddle tomorrow, and what we did today will look like one of your pink tea parties to what we got ahead of us."

It was rugged, broken country, mostly rock and drift sand, with some low-growing desert brush, and I lay awake for some time, speculating on our chances of getting through. Mostly, folks went by the northern route, following the old Government Road or Spanish Trail across the desert and over Cajon Pass. But with men following us with no good intent, it seemed best to risk the run to the south.

There was another pass down thataway, or so Joe Walker had told me. The Indians had used it a time or two, and some Spanish man had gone through the pass fifty or sixty years before. It was a risky trip, but we Sacketts always had an urge to try new country, and the time was right. As for that black-eyed woman . . . she should see some new country, too. Although I wasn't sure she was going to take to it.

A time or two I glanced over at Dorinda Robiseau. She lay quiet, resting easy, as she should have, for that bed of mine was a good one, and the sand I'd spread it on was deep and free of rocks, more comfortable than many a mattress. I could only see the white of her face, the darkness of her loosened hair.

She would be a trial in the days to come, but somehow I felt better just having her there.

It worried me, though . . . why were those men chasing her? And were they the law?

Remembering the men at the bar, I doubted it. They had a bad look about them. One thing was sure: if we faced up to each other out here in this lonely desert I was going to be glad that I was packing a gun.

That big-shouldered man who had stood with his back to me . . . he worried me. Why was there something familiar about him?

I awakened with a start, coming from a sound sleep to sharp attention.

Dorinda was sitting up, wide-eyed. "I heard something," she whispered.

"What?"

"I don't know. Something woke me."

My six-shooter was in my hand, and I looked first at the horses. They were standing heads up, looking off across the desert toward the east.

Rolling up, I put my six-shooter down carefully and shook out my boots—scorpions take notions to hide in boots and such like—and tugged them on.

A glance at the stars told me it was shaping up for daybreak. "Get up, and be very quiet," I said. "We're moving out."

She offered me no argument, and I'll give her this: she made herself ready in quicker time than I'd expected from any tenderfoot woman. By the time I'd saddled fresh horses, she had my bed rolled, and rolled good and tight.

Standing close in the dark, I said, "There's another spring not more than a mile over to the east. Sound carries far through a desert night."

Me, I wasn't altogether sure that whoever had made that sound was that far away, but it could be somebody searching for a waterhole.

We stepped into our saddles and I led off, heading due south, and keeping our horses in soft sand wherever I could. The Providence Mountains loomed high on our right, bleak, hard-shouldered mountains.

It was rugged going, but the night was cool and there was enough gray in the sky to enable a man to pick his trail. After riding about eight miles we left the rocks behind and had the Providence Mountains still on our right, with bald and open desert on our left, stretching away for miles toward distant hills.

"We're riding south," she said.

It was a question more than a statement, so I gave her the answer. "You want to get to Los Angeles, don't you? Well, I'm leaving the trail to them. We're going south, and then west through another pass."

What I didn't tell her was that I had only heard of that pass, and had only a rough idea of where it was. I knew that a stage line and a freight road went through that pass to the placer diggings around La Paz, on the Colorado.

The sky turned to lemon over the distant mountains, a warning that the sun would soon be burning over us. Somewhere to the south there were other springs, but I doubted if they would be easily found. The desert has a way of hiding its water in unexpected places, sometimes marked by willows, cottonwood, or palm trees, but often enough right out in a bottom with nothing but low brush around, and not a likely thing to indicate water. And we wouldn't have time to spend looking.

She rode up alongside me. "You're not a very talkative man."

22

"No, ma'am."

"Are you married?"

"If you're wonderin' about that scar on my cheek-bone, I got that in a knife fight in New Orleans."

"You have no family?"

"Me? I got more family than you could shake a stick at. I got family all over the country . . . only I am a lonesome kind of man, given to travel and such. I never was one to abide."

She looked at me curiously and, it seemed to me, kind of sharp. Then she said, "Where are you from, Mr. Tell? You hadn't said."

"No, ma'am. I hadn't."

We rode on for a couple of miles after that. A road runner showed up and raced out ahead of us, seeming glad of the company. Overhead there was nothing but sky, a sky changing from gray to brass with the sun coming up. Those mountains on our right, they were cool now, but within two hours they'd be blasting heat back at us.

"A few miles now, you keep your eyes open. We'll come up to a water hole, and I'd prefer not to miss it."

She offered no comment, and it was just as well. But she was a mighty pretty woman, and I'd have preferred riding easy with her, not worrying about folks coming up on me unexpected.

"You in some kind of trouble, ma'am?"

"I hadn't mentioned it," she said, coolly enough.

Well, that was fair. Only I was taking a risk, help-ing her this way.

It grew hot . . . and hotter. Not a breath of air stirred. The white sands around us turned to fire.

Heat waves shimmered a veil across the distance. We saw strange pools of water out there on the desert. Sweat trickled into our eyes. Our horses plodded along slowly; sweat streaked the gray film of dust that lay over them, and over us. Neither of us was of any mind to talk now.

From time to time I turned to look back, for we were out in the open, masked only by the shimmering heat waves and the wall of the mountain along which we rode. There was nothing behind us but heat waves and the far-off shoulder of mountain.

Cook's Well was some place along here, but we missed it, and I was of no mind to waste time in search. Blind Spring lay somewhere ahead, and if we missed that, there would be no water until Cottonwood, down at the end of the mountain chain.

Had they cut in after us? Or were they, as I hoped, riding west along the Government Road toward Marl Spring?

"It might make a lot of difference," I spoke out suddenly, "if I knew how anxious they were to find you."

She let her horse go on a few steps before she made answer, and then she said, "The man who is after me would kill you or a half dozen others to put his hands on me ... and then he would kill me."

Well, that answered that.

At high noon we drew up and I helped her down. I switched saddles and sponged out the mouths of our horses with water from a canteen. We each had a drink, and then we mounted up again and started on.

All the long day through we pushed on, and it was coming on to dark when I finally gave up on Blind Spring. We'd been too far out from the mountain or too close in, one or the other. The water in our canteens was low, and I hated to think what would happen if we didn't find water soon. We might make it, but the horses could not; and without the horses we would be helpless.

At dusk we halted and stripped the saddles from

our horses and I worked over them, rubbing them down, sponging out their mouths. Whatever Dorinda thought she wasn't inclined to say, nor was I inclined to listen.

The night came on, soft and dark, with the stars hanging easy in the sky. A cool wind blew up from somewhere, just a smidgin of it, but it felt good.

When I was finished with the horses I dug into my saddlebags for the last of the bread. It was hard and dry, but when I broke off a chunk and passed it to her, she tied into it like it was cake. We sat there on a sandbank, chewing away, and finally she said, "We're in trouble, aren't we?"

"It's like this," I said. "According to what I was told, from the point of the mountain we've got a three-cornered chance. Within three or four miles of this place there are three springs, they say, so we've a fair chance of locating one of them."

There was little time for rest, but trusting to the horses to warn us of any trouble coming, she rolled up in my bed and I hunkered down in the sand, working out a hollow for my body that came up on both sides of me, and there we rested.

In the morning, when I was pulling on my boots in the light of the last lone star, I saw Dorinda was awake, lying quiet, looking up at the star. "This country," I commented, "is hell on women and horses."

She did not turn her head or reply for several minutes, and then when I stood up to sling my gunbelt around my hips she said, "You get me to Los Angeles . . . that's all I ask."

I didn't answer her. With my bandana I carefully wipped the dust from the action of my pistol, checking the roll of the cylinder. She was asking a whole lot more than she knew, and right there I figured not to make any promises I couldn't keep.

When we had saddled up I said to her, "Just let the bridle alone. From here on, our horses might find water quicker by themselves."

Though I'd been told that Cottonwood was over the toe of the mountain from where we were, I decided to chance the other two springs, figuring there was no use wasting time in perhaps the wrong direction. So I headed south and let that stallion have his head.

For a while he plodded on, seeming uninterested in much of anything, but then a change in the wind brought his head up and he quickened his step, bearing off to the right toward what I guessed would be the Old Dad Mountains. But as we drew closer I could see there were two small ranges with a break between them.

In a little cove in the rocks we found a spring. There was a small trickle of water, and we let the horses drink their fill. After filling our canteens, we started on.

A dozen miles further along we found Willow Spring, with a good flow of water and some willows and a few cottonwoods around, most of them no bigger than whipstocks. Leaving Dorinda to freshen up, I took up my Winchester and hiked it to the crest of the ridge, where I could look over our back trail.

There was a flat rock that lay half in shadow, and down in front of it, about six to eight feet lower, a patch of white drift sand. Sitting on the edge of the rock where the shadow had cooled it off a mite, I studied our back trail toward the end of the Providence Range.

It was hot and still. Far off over the desert a dust devil danced among the Galleta grass and the creosote brush, but I saw no dust of human make. It could be we had shaken them. Maybe we would have no trouble after all.

What made me turn my head I'll never know, but glancing over my left shoulder I caught just a glimpse of a rifle muzzle as somebody drew sight on me.

Mister, I left off of that rock like I was taking a free dive into a swimmin' hole, and I hit that heaped-up sand on my shoulder and rolled over. When I came up it was on one knee, the other leg stretched out ahead of me, and my Winchester coming up to firing position.

The echo of at least two shots hung in the hot desert afternoon. I saw a man come around a rock and I tightened my finger on that trigger and made the dust jump on his jacket.

It was no great shooting, for he was no more than thirty yards off. I'd no idea where he'd come from, but one thing I did know. He wasn't going any place else. That .44 ca'tridge bought him a free ticket to wherever the good Lord intended, and I up and scooted down among those rocks, a-duckin' and a-dodgin' and a-squirmin' among rocks and brush, my shoulders braced for a bullet that never came.

When I hit the brush I was runnin' all out, and the next thing I know there's a squeal of startled irritation and there's that black-eyed woman holding her dress in front of her and starin' at me so fierce I had a notion to go back and face those guns. But I had another notion that beat that one altogether.

"Lady," I said, "unless you want to ride out of here naked, you'd better dress faster'n you ever did. They've come upon us."

A bullet spat sand over my boots and I rolled over in the brush and laid all flat out, peeking through the willow leaves for something to throw lead at. I saw nothing.

The echoes died away, and the afternoon was hot and still as ever. I'd no idea who was out there, or how many, but when they'd started shootin' at me they opened the ball, and I was going to call a few tunes my own self.

After a moment I eased back into the willows and went for the horses. They were out of sight among the rocks, and when I got to them I stood by, waiting for that woman to come up. While I waited I kept a sharp eye out for trouble and kept thinking about that range of hills to the south . . . all of four miles away, and all of it bald desert.

Nobody needed to tell me that whatever we did, we'd have to clear out of here. There was too much cover around from which these springs could be taken under fire. When that witch woman came out of the brush, her black eyes sparking fire, I didn't wait for any fancy talk. I just taken her up by the waist and threw her into the saddle and said, "Ride, lady!" And I went up into my saddle and we taken out of there like hell a-chasin' tanbark.

Somebody started shootin', and I caught time for one quick glance over my shoulder and saw there were four or five anyway, and then two more came up out of the ground right ahead of me. I shot into the chest of the first one, firing my Winchester one-handed, like you'd hold a pistol. The other one let fly at me and damned near busted my eardrums, and then my horse went into him. I heard him scream when a hoof smashed into his chest, but I only had time to hope that hoof wouldn't get hung up on the ribs.

Swinging wide to get that woman and the other horses ahead of me, I levered three fast shots back at those men, but I didn't hit anything but desert and rock. Ricochets have a nasty whine, though, and I caught a picture of the men duckin' for cover . . . and then all they could see of us was our dust.

We had good horses, and those men in tryin' to

sneak up on us had left theirs somewhere behind them. We were runnin' all out and reachin' for the shadow of the Bristol Mountains before I looked back and saw them come out of the hills, far back.

Closing in beside the Robiseau woman, I said, "Next time you take a bath it better be in Los Angeles."

three

It worried me that those men had come up on me from out of nowhere. Somebody in the lot of them was a tracker, or a shrewd one at judging what a man had in mind, and it left me uncertain of what to do. Having a woman with me complicated matters . . . or would if I let it.

Whatever they'd had in mind to start off with, it was a shooting matter now. There were three men down, and it was likely all three were dead, or hurting something fierce, and it wasn't likely the others would pull off and forget it.

Until now I'd been lucky—unlucky that they found us at all, but lucky in that I got off scot-free and didn't catch lead myself. Nor the woman or horses.

There was only one thing I could see to do, and that was to make them so miserable trying to catch us that they'd quit . . . if they had quit in them, which I doubted. So far it had cost them, but it was up to me to make it cost them more.

We crossed over the Bristol Mountains and headed due south for a pass in the Sheep Holes, thirty-five

or forty miles off, with not a drop of water anywhere between.

On the horizon, not far ahead of us, loomed the
black cone of a volcanic crater, and the black of a
lava field. Beyond lay a wide dry lake, and I pointed
our horses right at the spot where lava and dry lake
joined, and we rode on.

After a while, when we looked back, the notch in
the mountains through which we had come was gone,
vanished behind a shoulder of the mountain. There
was no sound, there was no movement but our own,
and the tiny puffs of white dust that lifted from the
face of the *playa* as our horses walked.

Behind us were shimmering heat waves, before us
and around us the air wavered, and changed the
looks of things. Small rocks seemed to tower above
the desert, and the sparse brush seemed to be trees.
Sweat streaked the flanks of our horses, dust rose
around us. We were in a lost world, shut out from
all about us by distance and by the shimmering heat.

Far off, something more than twenty miles away,
loomed a blue range of hills . . . the Sheep Hole
Mountains. Beyond them would be more desert and
more mountains.

Would they follow us? Or, wiser than we were,
mightn't they turn and ride right to Los Angeles,
knowing we would come there?

Only, of course, they did not know. We might go
to San Diego, or we might ride back north and go
to San Francisco along the coast road.

They had to follow, and before they caught up
with us I figured to lead them a chase. If they wanted
tracks to follow, I aimed to show them a-plenty, and
across some wild country. Only thing was, this black-
eyed woman wasn't going to like it. In fact, I figured
she regretted her bargain already. What waited her
when those men caught up with us, I couldn't say,

but it would have to be almighty bad to equal what lay ahead of us now.

Joe Walker and Old Bill Williams, mountain men both of them, had told me a good deal about the Mojave, but I'd learned of it from others as well, including a couple of Hualapai Indians I'd met in Prescott, both of whom had raided the ranchos for horses. It had been these Indians who told me most of what I knew of San Gorgonio Pass.

Desert travel was not new to me, for I'd crossed the cap rock of west Texas by the Goodnight-Loving Trail, and I'd been across the White Sands of New Mexico, as well as made a trip up the *Jornada del Muerto*, the "journey of death," so I was no tenderfoot when it came to deserts.

The desert can be a friendly place to a man on the dodge, but it is always better to hole up some place and wait for sundown. We were doing the worst thing a body could do in traveling by day, under a hot sun. The trouble was, those men back there behind us weren't about to give us any time.

Nobody knew better than me how lucky I'd been in that shindig back there, and it wasn't likely to happen that way again.

We pushed on, sagging in the saddle, the horses plodding steadily. Only me, I taken a look, time to time, to see if anything was gaining on us. Twice we stopped and I sponged out the horses' mouths and gave that Dorinda girl a mouthful of water to drink.

At sundown we could see mountains close ahead of us, and I began searching for the pass. One long arm of mountain had showed up to the east of us, and soon there was another on our right. A notch showed itself and I headed for that, glancing back one last time. There was a thin trail of something that might be dust, hanging against the sky.

In the cool dark, with a kit fox yapping somewhere up in the rocks, we rode through the Sheep Hole Mountains and made dry camp in a tiny cove.

Me, I was dead beat, and when I took that black-eyed Dorinda from her horse she could scarce stand, so I helped her to a place on the sand and kindled ourselves a hatful of fire and made coffee. Nobody needed to tell me how much she needed a hot drink, and I wasn't against the idea myself. Meanwhile, I checked out my Winchester, then my pistol. Rummaging around in my bedroll, I dug out a spare Colt, and made sure it was loaded, too.

"You killed a man back there," she said suddenly.

"Yes, ma'am. Maybe two or three."

"You don't seem bothered by it."

"They were comin' at me."

I poured out a cup of coffee for her and sat back on my heels, far enough from the fire not to be easily seen, and far enough from the crackle of the flames to hear if anything came upon us.

"I never had it in mind to shoot at any man, ma'am, but when somebody takes up a gun and comes for you in anger, he borrows grief. He was fetching trouble, so I gave him what he asked for."

She was half asleep already, and I passed her over a piece of jerked beef to chew on. "Go ahead," I told her, "it doesn't look like much, but there's a lot of stayin' quality in it."

After chewing a while myself, I said, "Carryin' a gun is a chancy thing. Sooner or later a man is put in position to use it. And a body has to figure that if somebody packs iron he plans to use it when the time comes; and if he draws it out, he plans to shoot."

I saw that she was fast asleep, so I covered her with a blanket and killed the fire. Then I went out and rubbed my horses down and gave them water,

just a mite squeezed into their mouths. It wasn't
much, and they wished for more; but it was all I
had to offer, and it's likely they understood.

Taking my Winchester, I prowled around, and
stood off under the stars, listening. This was spooky
country, with big Joshua trees hither and yon, any
one of which might be a man standing there. But
the desert night was cool, and mean-tired though I
was, it felt likely to my spirit.

Work and war never gave me much time for
poetry, but there was a man in my outfit during the
fighting near Shiloh who fancied it, and a time or
two he'd quoted things at me from a book he carried
in his shirt. I thought of it now, wishing I had some
of those words he used to speak of the desert night.

Sitting down on a rock, I sort of listened and
waited, studying the night with my ears, and each
sound held meaning for me. Sometimes I had to
sort the sounds a mite, but I knew what each one
was . . . and I heard no sound of man nor horse, no
creak of saddle, clink of metal, or brush of garment
upon stone.

That woman back there was done in. Like it or
not, we had to hole up somewhere and give her time
to rest, but the worst of it was, one of those men in
that outfit trailing us was a tracker and a hunter,
and a sight better than most. It was that man who
worried me, for if he continued to be as good as he'd
been so far, we would be facing a showdown a lot
sooner than I hoped.

More and more I wondered what I'd got myself
into, and what Dorinda Robiseau had done to make
them want her so much.

Not that she wasn't a beautiful woman, and the
kind of woman any man would want. Even now,
tired out as she was, she was lovely. But there was
more to it than that. And the chances were good

35

that I'd gotten myself on the wrong side of the law. Still, none of those men back at Hardyville had been wearing a badge . . . nor did they look likely to. Though all the men who wore badges through the western lands could not be said to measure up to a proper standard.

After a while I went back to our corner, checked the horses again, and burrowed into the sand to sleep.

But sleep did not come, dead tired though I was, for it came upon me that I knew mighty little about Dorinda Robiseau—not where she came from, who she was, nor where she planned to go. There was no telling about her, and all I had was my first suspicions that she was a witch woman.

Not that I place much stock in witches. All my life I'd heard tell of them, but I had never seen one, nor anything of their doings that I could swear to. . . .

Somewhere along in there, I sort of dropped off, and the next thing I knew it was daylight.

Broad, bright daylight . . .

The sun on my face awakened me, and I sat up fast and looked about.

A moment there, I couldn't place where I was, and then I saw the girl and she was a-settin' up, too.

"We slept over," I said, "and I was a fool to chance it."

About us the mountain walls lifted up steeply, in jagged, broken slopes. Up these a man on foot could climb, with some struggle and skill. Before us, and to the south, the desert lay open, masked only by a drift of sand, a pair of crowded Joshuas, and some small brush. On the horizon to the south, maybe twelve to fourteen miles off, were the Pinto Mountains.

The cove in which we were hidden comprised maybe an acre of flat ground and banked sand. There were some good graze plants in the bottom, and I had the five horses pegged out among them. Sand had heaped across the opening of the cove so that with the brush and all it was mighty near invisible from the outside, without a man riding up to the top of the sand hill.

It was that which saved us, that and the wind being so that none of the horses caught scent of one another. For when I went up to the top of the sand I could see those riders out there, not fifty yards away, and all bunched together, talking.

During the night there had been a wind stirring, not much, but enough to drift sand in this locality where it was loose, and our trail had drifted over. Evidently they had lost track of us and were talking it over to decide which was the most likely route for us.

The side of the mountain was drifted deep with that loose white sand. In some places it looked fit to bury whole sections of the range. So anybody taking a quick look our way would think there was nothing anywhere around but sand and rock.

Me, I motioned back to Dorinda to be still, and I lay there flat out on the sand with only the top of my head showing, and it screened by low brush and the base of a Joshua tree. My Winchester was with me, looking one-eyed at those men down there, ready to speak its piece if they started our way.

There was argument going on among them, but I could only guess at the words. Finally they turned and rode off toward the east and the spring at Twenty-Nine Palms.

That was the next worst thing to their finding us, because there was no nearer water that I knew of, and our canteens were shaking light with only mouthfuls of water remaining.

Lying there in the sand, I watched them ride off.

By the time they reached Twenty-Nine Palms they would figure it out that they were ahead of us, and the chances were they would sit right there by the water and wait for us, knowing that sooner or later we had to show up.

Oh, they would have it figured, all right! They would know about how much water we carried, and about how fast we used it, and right this minute they could guess within a quart the amount of water we had now . . . maybe closer.

So I watched them ride away, and I knew that, riding away in the direction we must go, they carried our lives along with them. It was no easy thing, seeing them ride off, knowing the girl behind me was depending on me for a way out; and when I thought of what tomorrow would bring—the sun, the dust, the miles upon miles of desert around—I felt fear.

But there was no sense in starting off into the blazing heat of a desert day. With them ahead of us, I could, for the first time, choose our time of travel. Taking up my rifle, I slid down the sand, and then walked back to where Dorinda was resting. From my expression she must have realized that trouble was upon us. She sat up, and, dropping to one knee on the sand, I told her.

There are men who prefer to keep trouble from a woman, but it seems to me that is neither reasonable nor wise. I've always respected the thinking of women, and also their ability to face up to trouble when it comes, and it shouldn't be allowed to come on them unexpected. Many a man has sheltered his wife from his troubles, until suddenly he dies and she awakens to poverty as well as grief. So I gave it to Dorinda hard and cold.

I drew her a diagram on the sand. "This here is Twenty-Nine Palms, and beyond is the San Gorgonio

Pass to the coast of the western sea. Right about there is Los Angeles."

"Aren't there other water holes? In some other direction?"

"More'n likely . . . but finding them wouldn't be easy."

She looked up at me. "We'll have to try, won't we?"

Simple as that. Sure, we'd have to try, because as well as I knew anything, I knew those men who had been trailing us would soon know they'd passed us somewhere and, as I'd thought when I watched them ride away, they would just wait for us there by the water.

Making some fire, I burned off the spines from some cholla and beaver-tail cactus and the horses ate them eagerly, for the pulp was moist. In Texas I've known ranchers to feed their stock that way. In this case, I was thinking more of the water they would get from it.

There was shade in the cove, and we sat tight, letting the day move slowly past. I'd made up my mind to travel no more by day, for, without anybody chasing us, there was no reason. Traveling in full desert sunlight can kill a man or a horse mighty quick without enough water . . . and we hadn't enough.

We did no talking, but I did a lot of thinking.

One time in Prescott I'd heard Paul Weaver yarning about some Mojaves who raided the California ranchos for horses and on their way back were driven from the trail by a sandstorm. With them was a Chemehuevi Indian who guided them to a hidden valley and a water hole in the canyon behind it.

This was in a country covered with Joshua trees and a weird lot of rocks piled up in all sorts of strange shapes. Near the valley there had been one

formation I remembered Weaver telling about—
he said it looked like a huge potato balanced on three
points of rock.

There had been two other water holes he mentioned, but of their location I knew nothing—only
that the Chemehuevi had known of them. It was
almighty little to begin with, and I was scared.

Twice I went back up to that ridge of sand and
looked off to the south, and neither time did my
looking give me any room for hope. All I could see
was miles upon miles of empty sand or burning rock,
mostly dotted with creosote bushes, or here and there
cactus or Joshua trees.

When the sun was almost down I put the saddles
on our horses, and loaded up our pack horse. Believe me, those horses were ready to go. They had
sense enough to know that if we were to get out
alive we had to travel. And so, with the dying sun
like a red ball of fire over the western mountains,
we rode over the sand ridge and headed south into
the empty, unknown desert.

After a while a bright star showed up, hanging
above the distant mountains, and I chose it for our
own, putting my horse's nose on it, and pointing it
out to Dorinda.

"What mountains are those?"

"I don't rightly know. Could be the Pinto Range.
There's a dozen small chains of mountains through
here . . . they all look alike the first time you see
them."

"You are risking your life because of me."

"Didn't figure on it."

Beauty does something for a woman—some of
them, anyway. Taking a side glance at Dorinda, I
could see that even out here she'd made an effort
to brush up and comb out. For a girl who'd been
riding and sleeping out, with no water and all, she

looked almighty pert. And I could imagine how I looked, a tall man with a big-boned, wedge-shaped face, a scar on my cheekbone, and by now a heavy growth of beard. Nobody ever claimed I was pretty, but by now I sure must look like an old grizzly coming out of hibernation. The only brushing up I'd done was to beat the dust off my hat and wipe my guns off careful.

Only two things a man really needs in this country to survive, a gun and a horse. . . . Come to think of it, though, there is something else.

Water.

Dorinda was thinking of it, too. She rode up beside me again and said, "However can we find water out there?"

"We've got to be lucky. In desert country you can find it up a canyon, or somewhere where the rock is faulted, or at the lowest point of a basin. But unless a body sees trees out in the bottom, I'd not chance that.

"Sometimes where a ridge pushes into the desert you'll find water, but mostly you look for trees or brush of a kind that needs water. Palm trees grow with their feet in the water and their head in the sun—that's what they say. It usually is only a little way to water if you see palms growing. Willows, cottonwood . . . they are good indicators, too.

"But you can't rely on that. Mostly a body should look for animal tracks, or birds flying, but mostly for bees. I've found that bees can lead a man to water faster than anything, but it's chancy . . . it's chancy."

I felt pretty sure there probably weren't five water holes within a hundred square miles . . . not that you could rely on. Tilting my hat brim down, I studied those hills. It was a cinch we weren't going to find anything this side of the mountains.

The night was cool. The stars hung bright above us, and the horses moved ahead, walking with a steady, distance-eating gait. Several times I opened my mouth and drank in great gulps of that cool air.

An hour passed, and then another. But the mountains seemed no nearer. We were out on the bare desert, and I worried over every bit of talk I'd heard of the Mojave, trying to recall anything that might be of help.

When, judging by the stars, two hours more had gone by, I drew up and got down, and helped Dorinda from the saddle. She was dead beat, I could feel it in her, and she sank onto the sand and just stayed there whilst I swapped saddles and talked encouragement to the horses. They were going to need it.

"How far have we come?" she asked.

"Maybe twelve miles, if you figure a beeline. More, by the way we've had to travel."

"How much further to the mountains? We'll rest then, won't we?"

"We won't rest until we find water . . . if we do."

She got up into the saddle again with some help from me, and we started on, only this time I walked. At least, I walked for the first couple of miles. When I began to stumble, as near asleep as awake, I climbed into the saddle myself.

Sometime after that, I dozed in the saddle, and when my eyes opened again the horses had stopped and it was gray in the east.

We had come up to a deep, sandy wash. Looking around, I saw that witch woman, looking like nothing but a tired girl, just sagging in the saddle and hanging on by sheer grit. My pack horse was gone.

Staring back over the desert, I figured I could see something back there, a black spot of something on the sand.

"You got anything in that outfit of yours that you can't afford to lose?" I asked.

She looked up at me, staring stupidly for a moment before the sense of the words reached her. Then she turned to look, and after a moment she shook her head.

"He may come on after us," I said. "It'll be in him to come after the other horses if he's able. They've been carrying more weight, but they're better stuff than him."

Looking up at her, I added, "Ma'am, you've got some solid stuff in you, too. You surely have."

But her lips were cracked and swollen, and there was no more spark to her than nothing. Nor in me, neither.

Right and left I looked, seeking a way through that wash. The banks were steep, and I feared to slide my horses down for fear they'd never get up after reaching bottom. At last I saw a place that looked like a broken-down bank, so I turned and headed for it. The sky was already lighter, and without water we would last no time in our condition if the sun caught us here.

We got through the wash, although I had to dismount and bully and harry the horses to get them up the opposite bank. A break in the mountains showed ahead of us, and I headed for it. From somewhere there came a burst of energy . . . most likely the last I had.

The sun was an hour old before we found shelter in the lee of a shoulder of rock. That horse of hers just quit cold, and I didn't blame him.

Dumping our saddle gear in the shade of the rocks, I stared around. There wasn't even a barrel cactus within sight, although this was the country in which they grew. Nor was there anything I could use to feed the horses or to give them a bit of mois-

43

ture. There was nothing but creosote, and mighty little of that.

Sizing up those horses, I could see they weren't going to travel much further, for they were used up. Two of them, the big stallion and my own original horse, might go on for a while. Even the second horse I'd bought from Hardy . . . but that was a question. We had to have water.

Dorinda had slumped over on the sand, but me, I walked out a ways from where she lay and studied the sand. For about an hour I crissed-crossed back and forth over the desert around and about, studying for tracks. Mighty few were to be seen, and none of them were bunched up and traveling the same route, which might indicate water.

Most desert creatures get along either without any water at all, or on mighty little, getting what moisture they need from what they feed on, be it plants or animals. But most will take water when they can get it, and some of them have to have it.

Finally I gave up and came back and sat down. I must have dozed off; when I woke up my throat was so parched I could scarce swallow, and when I tried to open my mouth I could feel my lips cracking with dryness. My tongue was like a stick in my mouth, and I knew our time was short.

The girl was asleep, or maybe passed out. I didn't look to see. One of the horses was stretched out on the ground, the others slumped three-legged, their heads hanging. My face felt stiff, and when I moved my eyeballs they seemed to grate in their sockets.

Catching hold of a rock, I pulled myself up and decided to try it one more time. And like before, I taken up a canteen and slung it around my neck where it couldn't slip off.

We'd slumped down at the foot of a great chunk of white granite, off by itself from the foot of the mountain. Others like it were around, and, starved for water though I was, I had sense enough to fix the shape of it in my mind . . . else I might never find my way back. Not that it was going to matter, if I didn't find water.

"I'll find water," I said out loud.

If she heard me at all, she gave no sign of it, but just lay there on the sand. So I turned and walked off.

The desert sand was white and hot, and the sunlight blazed back from the sand into my face and there was no shielding myself from it. After I had taken only a few steps I began to stagger. Once I fell against a rock and stood there for several mintues, I guess, before I got started again.

My eyes were on the sand, for I was hunting tracks. But something buzzed in my brain—something like an alarm bell of some kind—and then it was gone. Pausing, I felt my eyes blinking and I made my head turn, and there was a man standing on a rock some distance off.

As my eyes focused on him he lifted a rifle, sunlight glinted on the barrel, and he fired. Instinct made me grab for my gun, but the movement overbalanced me and I fell. That much I remember . . . and then nothing else for a long time.

Cold . . . I was cold.

Feebly, I tried to burrow into the sand for warmth, but warmth would not come. My eyes opened, and I tried to swallow. My throat was raw, and the membranes of it chafed and tightened with the attempt.

Somehow I got my hands under me and lifted myself up. It was night, it was cold, and it was very

45

dark. Stars were out, a chill wind was blowing . . . but I was alive.

Alive . . .

I started to crawl.

Suddenly a coyote yapped weirdly, not very far off, somewhere among the rocks, and I stopped.

When I started to crawl again something moved near me and something clicked on stone.

I knew that sound. A hoof . . . but not a horse.

Forcing my stiff neck to bend, I looked up and saw it there, black against the sky for an instant. A bighorn sheep. . . .

In the half-delirium that clouded my brain I felt irritation at the thought of the name. The bighorn was no more a sheep than I was. It was a deer. It had a body like a deer, hair like a deer . . . even the same color. Only the horns were different.

I crawled on, and the blood started moving within me. Pain awakened, I felt raw and torn inside, my body ached.

The bighorn would have to have water, so there must be water near. Forcing my muddled thoughts into line, I struggled to think more clearly. The bighorn had gone into the canyon, so the water must be there . . . at this hour he would be joining others of his kind at water, or would be leaving it.

Somehow I moved on, and then all movement ceased. Something stirred in me and I tried to move on, but I could not.

And then I felt the sun upon my back, and it was hot, terribly hot. My eyes opened and I struggled. In my mind was terror—terror of death, terror of dying here, like this. . . . And there was memory of the sheep. Pulling myself to hands and knees, I stared blearily around for tracks, and found none, for I had crawled upon the rock, bare rock where I saw not even the scars from hoofs.

Suddenly something buzzed by me and sang off into the distance.

A bullet? The sound lasted too long.

Struggling on, I paused again, hearing a queer, cricket-like sound. I knew that sound. It was the croaking made by the red-spotted frog.

And I knew something else. The life of that frog was lived in canyons or in places near permanent springs or seeps.

Water was near.

With a lunge, I came to my feet as though pricked with a knife point. Wildly, I stared around, and saw nothing.

And then that sound again . . . something buzzed by me that I knew for a bee. Quickly I started after it, taking three faltering steps before realizing that the sound had died away.

Scrambling and falling among the rocks, I came upon it suddenly—a basin in the white granite, filled to the brim with water . . . and it was no mirage.

I crawled down to it and splashed water into my face, then scooped a handful into my mouth and held it there, feeling the delicious coolness, and then the actual pain as some trickled slowly down my throat.

It seemed a long time that I lay there, letting that one gulp of water ease down my raw throat. And then after a bit I tried again.

The sun was blistering hot on the granite where I lay, so I crawled into the shade alongside the water. There was room to stretch out there. Several times I drank . . . once my stomach tried to retch.

When perhaps an hour had passed, I began to think.

The girl was back there . . . Dorinda. She and the horses . . .

But there had been a man who shot at me. Or had that been delirium?

Weakly, I struggled to sit up, and then I filled the canteen. I was going back.

I had to go back. I had to know.

four

My old tracks were on the sand to guide me, and I
found the place where I had fallen in attempting to
draw and return the fire of the man with the rifle.
There was a rock where such a man might have
stood, some distance off, but in plain sight. Around
where I had fallen there were no tracks but my own.

More carefully now—for it might not be delirium
that the man had shot at me—I moved among the
rocks of white granite toward the place. . . .

Gone . . .

Dorinda was gone, my horses were gone, my
packs and my gold were gone. Nothing was left.

There had been four or five riders, and they had
approached from the west. They had taken Dorinda,
my Winchester, my horses—and they had vanished.

They must have believed me dead. Here I was,
alone, on foot, and miles from any possible help.

Standing there in the partial shade of that rock,
I knew that I was in more trouble than I had ever
been in my life. I had a canteen of water and a
pistol with a belt of ammunition. But I had no
horse, no food, and no blanket. The nearest settle-

ment of which I knew was maybe a hundred miles away to the west—a Mormon town called San Bernardino.

For the moment my canteen was filled with water, and I had recently drunk. The tank that I had found in the rocks was a half-mile back up the draw; if I retraced my steps and camped there for the night I should have walked a mile to no purpose.

Pa, he always taught us boys to make up our minds, and once made up, to act on what we decided, and not waste time quibbling about. So I taken up my left foot and stepped out toward the west and followed it with my right, and I was on my way.

But I wasn't going far at midday, which it was by now. So I walked on from one of those islands of rock to another, sometimes resting in the shade a mite, then going on to another one, but always holding to the west. And away down inside me I began to get mad.

Until then I hadn't been mad, for we Sacketts, man and boy, are slow to anger, but when we come to it we are a fierce and awful people.

Another thing Pa had taught us boys was that anger is a killing thing: it kills the man who angers, for each rage leaves him less than he had been before—it takes something from him.

When that black-eyed girl back there at Hardyville asked me to help her get on to Los Angeles, I suspicioned trouble, but woman-made trouble, nothing like this. Now those men who chased after her had got her, and they had shot at me, left me for dead. They had taken my outfit and my gold.

Well, now, that was enough to make a body upset. Seemed to me this was a time for anger, and it came upon me. It was no wild, fly-off-the-handle rage, but a cold, deep-burning anger that pointed me at them like a pistol.

They would have gone to Los Angeles, but no matter. Wherever they had gone, I would find them.

A journey, somebody said, begins with one step, so I taken that step. I was started, and before I set my foot down for the last time on that journey there would be blood on the moon.

At sundown I struck out, headed westward. My life depended on getting to water before my canteen emptied. By now they had probably left the Palms, but that was away off to the north and beyond my direction now. I was going to hold westward, and hope.

A man afoot can walk a horse down. It has been done many a time, and while I had no idea of walking them down, if I could come up to water and find food I'd not be far behind them when they reached Los Angeles.

Food . . .

My stomach was already chafing my backbone from hunger, and my belly sure was thinking my throat must be cut, it had been so long since I'd eaten. Nonetheless, I just kept picking my feet up and putting them down.

We mountain boys were all walkers. Mostly it was the fastest way to get ary place back in the hills, for often a boy could cross a mountain afoot where no horse could go . . . if he owned a horse, or even a mule.

Westward the mountains lifted up maybe a thousand feet above the desert, but I'd crossed higher mountains, and if I couldn't go through, I'd go over.

Due west I walked, keeping a steady pace for upwards of an hour, then resting a few minutes and going on again. Two, three times I found rough going that held me up, but by moonrise I was close to the mountains and I picked out a narrow Indian trail or sheep trail. It showed white against the desert and between the rocks; I'd followed many such, and recognized it for what it was.

Most such trails are narrow, maybe four to eight inches wide, and usually easier to see from a distance than close up. I mean, from a cliff or ridge you can pick them out at quite a distance; but on the ground and close up they are hard to find, unless in regular use. But a body gets a knack for seeing them after a bit.

This one went south along the mountains, and I followed it for about a half-mile until it joined up with a westbound trail that cut into the mountains. Following it over and through the hills I found another spring at the foot of a granite spur that stretched out into a high mountain valley. The spring was marked by two patches of white granite, easy to see against the dark rock of the mountain.

In drift sand close by, I bedded down and made some sleep, after a long pull at the water in my canteen. Come daybreak, I drank from the spring, refilled my canteen, and took off to the westward while the sun was still below the horizon.

It came on me then if I was to eat I'd have to look sharp, or maybe lay out near a water hole of a night and try to kill something that came for water. A sheep would be best, but one more day without grub and I'd tackle a desert wolf or most anything that walked or flew—or crawled, for that matter.

It was about then that I came up to the horse tracks.

There must have been fifty in the lot, maybe more, and they were pretty well strung out. These were not wild stuff, but shod horses, most of them, and they were driven. As near as I could tell, they were driven by two men.

Right away I took to the rocks to study it out. The way it seemed to me, this was no country for an honest man to be driving horses. There were no ranches anywhere within miles, and no occasion for anybody to be moving a herd through here that I could grasp hold of. Anybody moving horses would be likely to keep to well-traveled trails and known water holes.

Then I recalled Old Bill Williams, and what Joe Walker had told me about the characters from Arizona who used to steal horses in California and drive them across the desert to sell in Arizona . . . or the other way around. Maybe somebody was still doing it.

Horses meant water; and wherever these horses were going, it was a place known to the drovers, who were heading them right across country *toward* something.

That something must mean a hide-out, a camp. And that meant grub. It also could mean a horse for me.

Hunkered down among those big old rocks, I gave study to the problem. If the men driving the horses were thieves, they wouldn't take it kindly of me to come upon them, and they might start blasting at me with firearms. Nevertheless, they would have grub, which I needed, and they would have horses.

For maybe a half-hour I held my place, and gave the time to studying the country around. You never saw such a jumble of boulders, heaped-up rock, and cactus in your life.

And then of a sudden I recalled what I'd been told about a balanced rock near a Hidden Valley, a rock like a huge potato. For there, not more than a few hundred yards off, was just such a rock.

The trouble was, in a jumble of rocks such as that

a man might look for years and not find the entrance to the valley unless he was mighty lucky, or found some tracks. And there was likely a lookout somewhere up among the rocks. No matter—I had to take my look.

Right at that moment I didn't much care. I was hungry, and I was dead tired, and I had been put upon by the men hunting that woman. They had taken my outfit and they had left me for dead, and before this thing was over they would pay through their hides.

So I started to follow those tracks.

"You huntin' something?"

The voice came out of nowhere. I was smart enough to freeze right in my tracks, and when I looked up I saw a man standing there with a Winchester aimed at my belt buckle. He was a rough-looking character wearing a flat-brimmed hat and beat-up chaps.

"You're damned right I am," I said irritably. "I'm hunting three square meals and a horse."

He chuckled at me. "Now you don't tell me you come all this way afoot?"

"No," I said, "I been set afoot. And when I get up in the middle of a horse I'm headed for Los Angeles to find those who left me."

"You a Los Angeles hombre?"

"Arizona," I said. "I started over here to buy horses and goods to take back, and in Hardyville I ran into this woman."

He lowered his rifle. "You don't look like the law," he said, "so come along. We can feed you, anyway."

He walked over to some rocks and he said, "You've got to crawl." He indicated a hole where two rocks sort of leaned together, and I got down

54